PEARL
〰〰〰 AND HER 〰〰〰
GEE'S BEND QUILT

Thank you for keeping the Gee's Bend
legacy alive!

[signature]

Published in the United States by Pen Legacy Publishing, a division of Pen Legacy, LLC, Philadelphia, PA. www.penlegacy.com

Library of Congress Cataloging – in- Publication Data has been applied for.

Hardback ISBN: 978-1-7358-7985-7
Electronic book ISBN 978-1-7357-5123-8
Paperback ISBN: 978-1-7357-5122-1

PRINTED IN THE UNITED STATES OF AMERICA.

Illustrated & formatted by: India Sheana
Photography by: Olivia Ball (Quilt page 37)

First Edition

THIS BOOK BELONGS TO:

_____

Dedication

You are the great granddaughters of Pearlie Kennedy Pettway and Jensie Lee Irby. You are the granddaughters of Forida Mae Irby and Phyllis Marin. You are heirs of a rich history that spans multiple continents. A story, yet to be told truly, that is cultivated with the blood, sweat and tears of those who came before you. May the footprints of our ancestors propel you to dream the unthinkable, guide you to your true calling and keep you in the path of your grandmother's prayers. Camille and Camryn Irby, you are my forever loves!

Always,
Your Favorite Aunt in Connecticut

On a lazy Sunday afternoon, Pearl sat playing in the living room with her friends Sallie and Ella as the aroma of homemade biscuits, smothered chicken, rice, collard greens from the garden, and Grandma's famous teacakes filled the house.

"Wow, that quilt is amazing," Sallie said. "My mom has quilts like this at our house."

"Grandma told me I come from a long line of Gee's Bend quilters whose quilts have been displayed in galleries and museums all over," Pearl proudly boasted. "When I get older, I'm going to make quilts, too. And one of my quilts will hang over there one day." Pearl pointed to the empty space where she intended to display her work.

"That's pretty neat. But what are Gee's Bend quilts? I've never heard of that before," Sallie asked, wide-eyed.

Pearl sat up straight, with confidence. "Back when my grandma was younger, the house she lived in did not have any heat, so she and her siblings used quilts to keep warm during winter. The families who lived in Gee's Bend, Alabama were very large. Some had ten or more children, so they needed lots of quilts.

They would tear up old clothing to use for fabric. The women would move from house to house, quilting during the evening. During the day, many of them worked at the Freedom Quilting Bee. They would use sewing machines to piece together the tops, but they quilted them together by hand."

Sallie and Ella listened in amazement, surprised that their playdate had turned into a fantastic lesson about Pearl's family history.

"Grandma always says, 'Quilts are like your handwriting,'" Pearl explained. "She says every quilt should be different from everyone else's. I asked Grandma how she comes up with so many different designs. She told me she talks to God when she quilts, and He gives her an idea every time. I told her that I am not sure that I will be able to quilt the way she does but she told me, 'You can only do your best. You cannot do my best.'"

"Helping Grandma is exciting," Pearl tossed her hands in the air with a sweet smile. "I get to pick the pieces of fabric that she will use next or thread the tiny needle. Sometimes, I thread 3 or 4 so they will be ready when she needs them."

Sallie and Ella lay on their bellies as Pearl recounted the rest of her story, her voice rising and falling like she was singing a song. "Grandma says quilting isn't always easy. Sometimes the fabric is very thick, and she has to use a thimble to keep from pricking herself. One time she stuck herself, and I could tell she was vexed. But no matter what, Grandma keeps quilting."

"It sounds like your grandma
knows what she's doing," Ella said.
"I bet you can't make one!"

"Yes I can," Pearl blurted in response to Ella's challenge. "Since you think you know everything, listen to this."

"The most important part of the quilt is the top. To make her special designs, Grandma sews many different scraps together. Sometimes, she uses my old clothes that don't fit anymore or grandpa's old t-shirts." Pearl spoke quickly, telling everything she learned, but paused to take a breath before starting again.

"When the top is finished, the rest of the quilt is ready to be stitched together. Did you know that?"

Pearl crossed her arms in satisfaction when Sallie and Ella shook their heads, then went on.

"The middle layer is called the batting. When Grandma was little, sharecroppers grew the cotton and they would pick, then flatten it for the quilts. Next comes the backing. Quilters used to use 25 lb. flour sacks for the backing, but now we can go to the store to buy everything that we need."

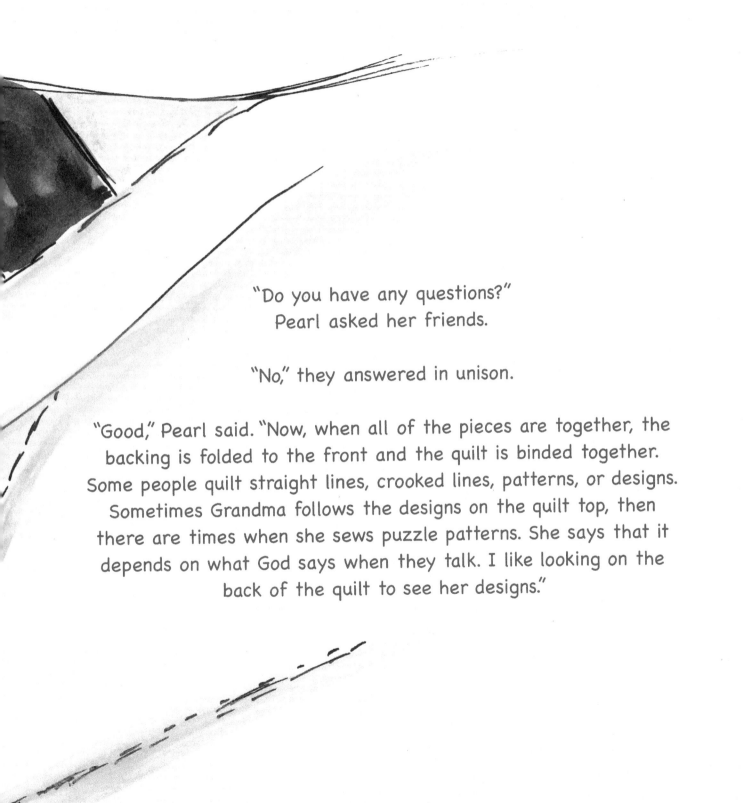

"Do you have any questions?"
Pearl asked her friends.

"No," they answered in unison.

"Good," Pearl said. "Now, when all of the pieces are together, the backing is folded to the front and the quilt is binded together. Some people quilt straight lines, crooked lines, patterns, or designs. Sometimes Grandma follows the designs on the quilt top, then there are times when she sews puzzle patterns. She says that it depends on what God says when they talk. I like looking on the back of the quilt to see her designs."

"Wow, Pearl, you are right," Ella exclaimed. "You know a lot about quilting. Grandma says that me and my cousins need to learn so that the world will know about our quilts, too."

The girls hadn't noticed that Grandma sneaked in to eavesdrop and hear Pearl teaching her friends so well. She held a few quilts in her arms as she addressed the girls with a sweet smile.

"It sounds like Pearl has been watching and listening." Grandma beamed with pride. "She knows all about our family quilts and where they came from. We didn't have a lot of money back then, but we always had our quilts. Our elders gave us quilts as gifts, especially when we moved up north. We got them when we married. We even got them when we came back down south for visits. Ella and Sallie, I have a gift for you. Here are your very own Gee's Bend quilts. Take good care of them."

Grandma handed each girl a quilt, and was delighted to hear them squeal with excitement. "On the back of your quilts, I have signed my name and written the name of the quilt. No one else has a quilt like yours. One day, you can pass it down to your own children and tell them the story of Gee's Bend quilts."

About the Author

Tangular A. Irby is an author, educator and quilter. She holds a BS in Business Administration, a Masters in the Art of Teaching and a 6th Year in Educational Leadership. Her love of children's books developed during her time as a second grade teacher, believing the power of a good book can never be overstated. She has worked professionally with all grade levels, Pre-K through 12. Most recently, she has worked in higher education. Growing up, Tangular admired the beauty of the quilts gifted to her by family. Eventually, quilting became a way to honor the legacies of her maternal and paternal grandmothers – both Gee's Bend quilters, who passed on long before their creations were recognized as more than just a means to keep their families warm.

About the Quilter

This book is based on the artistry of Mary Leathea Pettway. Born and raised in Alberta (Gee's Bend), Alabama, Mary L. is a child of God, loving wife, mother and grandmother, who continues to be an active member of the small rural community. Mary L. puts God first and is not ashamed to praise Him anytime or anywhere for everything He has gifted her.

For quilt inquiries
or additional information contact:
Learningadvantagenetwork@gmail.com